Loose Lips

Also by Ray Clift and published by Ginninderra Press

Fiction

The Journey of Hamlyn Baylis Wells

Always In Denial

Smithy's Cupboard

Shaken & Stirred

Shalom Samuel

The Last Journey of Hamlin Baylis Wells

She Walks the Line

The Journeys of Hamlin Baylis Wells

Smithy & Suzie

Three in One

The Publisher

The Publisher's Acronym

Non-fiction

Maybe Blue Ghosts

It's a Fine Line

Cops, Crooks, Courts & Spooks

Ray Clift

Loose Lips

Thanks to
My family and friends, who are always are there.
Sharon Kernot and Gary MacRae – a support team.
Eric Van Krussen – my lawyer friend from the courts.
But not the least, Stephen and Brenda Matthews, who
own the excellent Ginninderra Press, for without them
us local writers would still be lost in some ether, unable to
read our adventures in the realm of the art of writing.

Loose Lips is fiction, so it is said – but is it? There is a lot
of actual and traceable history within the story. A slogan
used in World War Two was 'Loose lips sink ships.'

Loose Lips
ISBN 978 1 76041 605 8
Copyright text © Ray Clift 2018
Cover photo © Ginninderra Press

First published 2018 by
GINNINDERRA PRESS
PO Box 3461 Port Adelaide SA 5015
www.ginninderrapress.com.au

Prologue

Melbourne, 1985

The voice on the telephone appeared to be sharp and peremptory, but I didn't hear too well what it said, partly because I was only half-awake and partly because I was holding the receiver upside down. I fumbled around and grunted, 'James Newton.'

'James,' said my boss, the editor of Melbourne's biggest newspaper.

I gathered my senses, after the night before's whisky-filled mess. 'Yes, Bill, sorry about the delay. Haven't yet had my favourite beans. What's up?'

'I know it's your day off but I need you to come in soon. Is that okay?'

I knew it was not a question, it was a command and journo jobs are precarious at this time.

'Of course' were his last words before he hung up.

I struggled out of bed, shaved, showered and nuzzled my third cup in rapid time, and thought about Sue (my sometime girlfriend) who wasn't here any more to get me going

I caught the tram, due to a broken fan belt on my old Holden ute.

Fifteen minutes later, I was in the slow lift with a young journo who had rejected a small date offer a few weeks ago. Snotty bitch. Maybe I ought to drop one of my smelly farts, but I hesitated – one day soon, she might be my boss.

Bill greeted me with a warm man's handshake and a bubbling coffee pot. I sat in the comfortable leather lounge and waited for him to open up.

'OK, James, look at these.' He pushed a couple of flight tickets towards me.

I picked them up and saw that the destination was Burnie in Tasmania. There were bookings for a hire car and for two nights at a motel. I looked up as he was leaning back and saw that he had the latest shiny RSL badge on his lapel and was wearing one of his best Italian grey suits. I liked him. He was straight and not one for wordy conversations, getting straight to the point. He reminded me of my granddad.

A long pause gave me time to wonder about the trip and the second ticket, which might have been for anyone who wanted to come on the trip.

I knew a fair bit about Bill. I'd done my research. I watched him on the television when he was a war correspondent with the lot. The flak jacket, the helmet, the steady voice, and him occasionally ducking when a shell went overhead in the last months of the Vietnam conflict. He was there when the enemy took the city of Saigon and people rushed to the harbour just to be free, though many could not escape. He won an award for that and after he was wounded the Yanks gave him a Purple Heart. I wonder if he ever met the soldier who Robin Williams played in that movie.

I knew Bill was happily married with grown kids and he was aware I was divorced and that I miss my kids. He may have tracked that far because he knew I was in commerce but when the marriage went west I did a journo course and here I am – a freelancer. I had the trick of being able to let my thoughts run and still pick up the nitty-gritty required for a mission so I had that look on my face of absorbing what I was being told. Maybe Bill had it as well because we were really on the same plane in many areas.

'Anthony Jones is about eighty-seven and still creates great art out of driftwood, which he collects at Land's End on the western tip of the island. Heard of it?'

Not wishing to let him know of my ignorance, I mumbled, 'I think so,' which caused a wry smile on Bill's face.

'Does the name ring a bell?'

I scratched my head and loosened some dandruff which fell onto the desk and the immaculate Bill passed over a brush and dustpan for me. For Bill, everything has a place and dandruff is not a part of his great crop of white hair.

Then, as if on cue, my right frontal orb started to work and the words burst forth. 'Was he the oldest protester in 1983 at the Franklin Dam with Bob Brown? Got locked up.'

'Yep, but there's a lot more to this man than just a protester. My sources tell me he was a brilliant student. Joined the army in the Engineering Corps, was involved in demolition. Was with Army Intelligence and seconded to the Brits, just before the outbreak of war. From then on it's fuzzy, and he may not want to talk about it. He was decorated with a few good medals, like a DCM for starters. If you can perhaps raise his MI5 service, it would be great. And of course you served in Vietnam.' He waited for a response. He got one.

'Why would that loosen his tongue?'

'His son, his only child, was killed in that war.'

I was thoughtful and wondered whether it might open more wounds. I asked if he was on his own. 'He might not open up. Remember, loose lips sink ships.'

'Wife died with a broken heart some time ago. I don't think the Secret Commissions Act would apply now, but there may be be some men in black suits hovering around. Keep an eye open.'

'Bloody spooks. OK, boss, when do I fly out?'

'Fourteen hundred hours tomorrow. The car will be there when you arrive but stay for the night. Then drive down to Arthur River. He has a shack there.'

We shook hands and I left.

There was the bitch in the lift, so I let go a loud fart this time. She held her nose and got out on the next floor while I laughed. Imagine her going to interview this old fellow.

*

It all went to plan. I had a great sleep and, apart from winning a couple of hundred bucks on the pokies that night, I was ready to set off to the Arthur River. I enquired about my interviewee before I left. Everyone said 'Chocko From Morocco', which increased my curiosity.

I remembered the only close male in my life as a kid – not my father, whose memory over time I'd blocked out – but granddad Frank. He had a PhD and I guess my skill as a wordsmith was inherited.

He ruminated to me when he was in a hospice. 'Do humans ever consider life while they live it? Every minute? No. The saints and poets maybe. they do sometimes, I expect. Sadly, closer to my death now, I look back on my life and recognise the tragedies of small splendours, lost each day, when I anxiously scurried to and fro so fast with no time to look at and smell the roses. More money, more things, more friends, more accomplishments: the list is endless. More complaints, more recognition, more respect, just more, more, more. I don't really know who I am, and I am about to pass to another world. An Angel might ask, "Who are you?" Perhaps I just shrug. Maybe I'm like a military map with overlays which were peeled off as the war moves along. I'm reminded of the book by Oscar Wilde, *The Face of Dorian Gray*. I feel a deep need to be, to do more than I could possibly handle. It is not the work which eventually kills us, but the way we give it such meaning and let it control our lives, Thank God I'm off the treadmill, but it took a long time. I'm happy to pass over.'

The hostie came around just after the plane took off to Tasmania. with a tray full of Arnott's biscuits. I remember when I opened a tin at home. I loved the chocolate ones and sneakily grabbed a handful. But Mum set traps and never spoke about it at the time.

Then one day in front of relatives she found the occasion to expose me. 'I think we have a mouse in the house called James.'

I hung my head in shame, unable to study the faces of people who really knew of some of my mother's nuances. I understand now that in her childhood things were tough.

But when she was not around the oldie aunties said, 'It's okay, James. We're all onto to her.'

We all knew in the weekly Monopoly games that she always slid some cards onto her lap. She also pinched flower cuttings from the Botanical Gardens until she was caught by the head gardener and they banned her. She never got over it. And her Methodist ladies group used to make a joke of it.

Funny how flights dredge up old memories.

1

Chocko From Morocco

He was old all right, I saw when I met him on the rise towards the shack, carrying an armful of new driftwood. But he was a long way from feeble. His neatly parted white hair was a contrast to the dark body and his face. I had expected someone who would look like a kangaroo in a tuxedo. I was wrong on that score, and on many others. His roman nose showed no sign of falling off with a skin cancer. It was long and veined

His lined face showed years of sun and I could see why some called him 'Chocko'. I still had to find out about 'Morocco'. I guessed it was something to do with the war, but I might have been well off the mark. Surprisingly his ears were a pink colour, which I guessed was the Anglo-Saxon blood somewhere in his arteries. One of his ears held a plastic button indicating hearing loss. His voice was thin and dry and sounded like rustling bamboo leaves.

Who am I to judge, was my immediate thought and I wonder ed what I would look like if I ever reached my mid-eighties. I am much older in body and spirit after my survival from Vietnam. He must have found out about my service and instinctively knew about my decline. He might have read about all of us and how we suffer from PTSD, because he lost his only son. I am part of those unwanted creations from a lost war, with a gammy leg and the promise of a Veteran's pension. And now on my own.

My prospects of a long life aren't too good. Perhaps I'll find my

Arthur River somewhere, waiting for me, and the great boulders whispering, 'Come sit on me in the sun, and watch the fish swim.'

Talking of boulders, Chocko leaned on one and took a deep breath before we strolled the several yards to the shack. On the way, I saw the lovely Arthur River come into view and could understand how people would want to live in this pristine area.

Inside the shack. it occurred to me in a flash that this could be a time to go for the simplest lifestyle, instead of a constant string of antidepressants and constipation, which comes with all of those pills, potions and creams. It was time for me to absorb the way which Chocko lived. Maybe with his welcome he was honouring me with a home-made meal, as I hear and see the pot bubbling with the aromas of garlic and other herbs, permeating the atmosphere inside the shack. He invited me to relax in a comfortable chair, and listen to the cracking fire, and the pot on the old Metters stove.

Meanwhile, he chatted about his love of Arthur River. 'You can see that it's surrounded by dense rainforest and named after the wild river that runs from the mountains to the sea. The river's a great base for exploring the Tarkine wilderness, Tassie's largest tract of temperate rainforest. On the drive here, you saw the tiny township which is the northern entry to the Western Explorer roadway that leads from the coast to the wilderness area. There's a plaque titled "The Edge of the World" which is lashed by winds. This coastline is beautiful and remote and suffers from the Roaring Forties winds, creating a churning effect at the river's mouth that deposits ancient logs and driftwood on the beach. That's where I collect the materials for my art hobby. The area's popular with four-wheel drivers, sadly. There's a population of around twenty-five who enjoy the peace and comfort. I know most of them. They usually stay in the summer months. There are great campsites, holiday homes with picnic and barbecue facilities available and also there's a local tavern. It's a two-hour drive from Burnie, as you know.'

I just relaxed, and gazed at the brown walls with patterns of flattened leaves and as my eyes soared, I saw the colour photos of the sacred heart of Jesus and cross. The Virgin Mary was dominant. These were the beloved relics of his wife.

He stirred the pot and put out home-made bread on the well made Tasmanian oak, table which when brushed gave off an earthy aroma, after all of those years.

He smiled with a toothy show of white teeth and I could see a flush of excitement forming across his face, with the deep grooves telling a story of each pivotal moment in his long life. For me, an undiscovered story lay within the walls of the shack. I needed to explore in depth the albums on the walls and the blank space between them.

'The blank space, son –' he started to call me that, as if I was his only child, whose helicopter ride had ended in some mysterious rice paddock, his remains later returned to his homeland. He pointed to the blank space. 'This one was our favourite photos because she glowed, but it makes me sad if I stare at it too long. But enough of that. Come, come with me to the workshop – it's my pride and joy.'

And we moved into the huge workshop, thrice the size of his two bedrooms and kitchen. On the way in, he dropped the latest pile of driftwood and walked to the old Granma phone with its oiled wood and pedestal.

'Still works, James.'

I picked up the old 33rpm records and plucked out the movie soundtrack of *Casablanca*, the movie made in 1942.

He looked at me. 'Did you ever see the movie, son?'

I shook my head but knew all about it. It was apparently his wife and his mother's favourite movie as someone had scrawled in ink, 'the very best'. I put the record down and felt I was on the verge of some secrets.

'I'll tell you the story about that tomorrow, son. Meanwhile, can you bring in the two bowls of stew and I have a bottle of great port if you drink that.'

I nodded and took the bowls into the workshop. I started to eat and enjoyed the meal with the bread, which I dunked, something I hadn't done since the war.

He was holding up a large piece of driftwood, stroking it as if it would take on legs. Without looking at me, he started to talk. 'My Mum was French, as you may know. She taught me three languages which I can still use: French, Spanish and a smattering of German.'

He turned round, eyes blazing with anger – not towards me but, I believed, the German race. The silence that followed took on a life of its own and magnified, while he breathed deeply and stood thinking.

I reached out to him be brushed me away and was soon back to his normal, calm exterior. I knew then that there were deep memories not expunged from his soul, and I hoped to help him. I would be his exorcist.

But before that trial he wanted to talk about his parents. I saw a photo on the wall of a Light Horseman and written underneath was 'Corporal Benjamin Jones in Egypt 1916. Born in Burnie, Tasmania. Part of the old Welsh mob. Old Uncle William came here as a convict. Another miner and a carpenter.'

The plot thickened. A convict – maybe a ticket of leave man. I couldn't wait to hear the early history of the Jones family.

'I can guess, son, that you're curious about the thirty-something period, but before that I'll share some of my recollections of when I was in my early teens. Dad taught me to drive in that early age in the bush. We kids were driving tractors, trucks, riding on motorbikes and generally mucking around until the local cop gave us a thick ear, with the well known warning, "Wait till your father gets home," which caused a fair bit of consternation to some kids, whose fathers were wife and child bashers, taking out all their terrible traumas on their loved ones, which Dad never did – he despised woman bashers.

'Occasionally we heard about dads who were killed in mine explosions, and those who either used a .303 or a rope to escape all their troubles, especially in the downturn with the Great Depression.

'Dad and I had some Keystone Cop moments with the poor old ute hitting potholes, back wheels skidding and engines racing wild and cranky. Dad didn't shout out but he gave me the eye-roll of the century with his eyes wide open like the bottom of a bottle of Johnny Walker

Black Label. I giggled and it was infectious, because he laughed as well, so loud his bladder gave up, spilling drops on the seat. He looked like a drill sergeant with his fly button undone but quickly regained his usually well known composure and yelled out, "Bloody Japanese bladder." When it was done, he always said, "Don't tell Mum." But she knew, as she was always peering out of the curtains and probably had a great laugh as well.

'I was doing well at school. Scouts came, then cadets followed, along with the CMF. Then my lucky day came when I was recruited into the small regular army in the Engineer Corps. I picked up some clues about Intelligence. Got two pips, after a lot of training. But another pivotal moment came along.

'Turn up the volume on the tape, James.' A command rather than a request.

'I listened to Dad's good advice in 1934. "Time for marriage. Search for a suitable mate. Avoid widows and unmarried mums with lots of snotty kids to inherit – they're looking for a patsy with a bank roll to spend – or you'll end your days sucking grog at the RSL with all those wounded ex-servicemen, spilling the beans about their terrible life, with a nagging woman and kids, who ran away with the travelling salesman." Dad was true to this word. If he went to the RSL, it was a couple of glasses and a quick retreat before another ear wax borer bobbed up, as he used to say.

'I reacted to my Dad's words in an affirmative manner and started the search, not that there were too many women about as most had grabbed any bloke wearing an army tunic.'

'How did the search go? Did you have to move to Launceston or Hobart?' I asked Chocko.

'Two questions there, son. No big-time girls, just the local dance, which I went to more frequently after I had some dancing lessons. I met up with my oldest crush from school. We dated as much as we could and in 1935 I proposed to Mary. Can you stop for a while, James, while I fix the bandsaw?'

He returned to his story. 'Right. We married soon after and went to Sydney for our honeymoon. Great days. Mary knew what could happen in war because her Dad was gassed in the big one, lost a lung, and died in misery.'

'Where do we go from here, Chocko?'

'Paul was born in 1936 during the lead-up to World War Two. Not brown like me, just a gold tan like his mum, and like my mum Jane, who was a descendant of the Plantagenets who ruled England for three centuries with their wealth and their red-gold hair – and never spoke a word of English. As to Paul, he was doted on by many of the Jones fold and friends.

'Duty came first and I was going so well in the Intelligence Corps that I was seconded in 1938 to England, and it was a sad farewell. Mary would have to cope on her own, for a long time. Just when I was about to take leave, 1939 came on. England and the world were embroiled in that conflict. 1940 saw the Battle of Britain. I was able to duck home for a short time in 1941.

'The Jones mob gained a third generation of soldiers when Paul went into the engineers when he was eighteen years of age, but I'll tell you more about that later.'

2

Jane

'Dad described my mother Jane to me, as if time had stood still. There was a range of emotions from pleasure to comedy. We were fishing in the Arthur River, just a stone's throw from my half-built shack. The time and the setting were in Hastings, after his wounds from the charge of mounted soldiers, and at a time when soldiers were recovering with some fun at the local dance hall.

'She was quite a doll, with a hint of a French accent. She wore a white belted raincoat, no hat, a well styled head of platinum hair, boots to match the coat, a pair of blue-grey eyes that looked at me as if I said a dirty word. I helped her off with her raincoat. She smelled great. She had a pair of dancer's legs, so far as I could determine, that were not painful to look at. She wore sheer stockings. I stared at them intently, especially when she crossed her legs and held out a cigarette to be lighted. "Top-shelf make-up," I ruminated. I think she was second guessing my thoughts all the way, with me sniffing around her with flared nostrils.

'I broke the atmosphere with a comment. "You're wearing a lot more today." I snapped the lighter for her.

'She looked at her watch. "It's too early for unwanted passes." And then she saluted me. A fast about-turn followed. She looked back with a wide smile, showing even white teeth. Be here next Saturday."

'He told me about his many sleepless nights in the long wait till Saturday.'

'What did he say, Chocko?' I asked.

'He said he was drifting along like a boat at its moorings, madly rowing but getting nowhere and then he realized that the jetty rope was still attached. The changing winds and the currents controlled which way h should go.'

'Great metaphor, Chocko.'

Chocko nodded. He stroked a piece of twisted driftwood, and I guessed his creativity ran in parallel with his flashbacks.

'We're now at the stage when Dad got the pluck to hint at a proposal. Time ran away in those days and marriages came quickly, because of soldiers in danger of death and disablement. Saturday had passed and marriages celebrated in the hall were frequent. The couple were drawn together with the prospect of leaving a bombed-out country, and going to a place with warmer climate without war on its shores. Peace and quiet was yearned for by all the population.'

'I recall him telling me, "I was nervous as the straight man in a knife-throwing act. My mouth throbbed with a dull red pain, like a devil's toothache. Jane knew I was on a roll but stuck like that boat tied to the jetty. She said, 'Spit it out, man.' I fumbled with the ring and dropped it on the dance floor. I found it resting up against the pianist's foot. He was bashing the keys and singing, 'Roses are blooming in Picardy'. Stuff Picardy, I thought. I spoke a couple of sorries as I crawled out from under his feet and held the jewel tight. I ran around looking for Jane, just like an unregistered dog, and there she was, leaning on the balcony, smoking and watching the waves lap around the pylons. She turned round and said, 'Of course I'll marry you, Benjamin, you big clod. Take me far away to your Tasmania.' The hall had another celebration the next Saturday, with her teary parents and others. Many soldiers formed an arc and off we went, in the neighbour's old Ford to the hotel rooms."

'I was born in 1918. By 1919 we were safely back in Tasmania, missing the terribly flu epidemic in 1920. Dad was working in the mines at Mount Bischoff, while Jane and I were set up in Burnie. Jane was the popular dressmaker in the town. And the best dancer. The family made a great fuss over me. Dad remarked when he first saw me, "Brown as an old wombat." It was not long before I had a series of nicknames. Chocko finally stuck.'

3

Mount Bischoff

'Take a look at the map and you'll find the mine.'

I spotted it and held my finger on it, while he adjusted his hearing aid. I watched him while he tapped a few times on his breast pocket to raise the volume. It came on and he started to speak again.

'I was deaf long before they invented these doovers, son. It's my fault – too close to noisy circular saws and working too many shifts. And these days, I keep dropping the doover in the mud. I did all those shifts to put in the bank. I'm not destitute now – I still have some money in a bank in England. I'll tell you later down the track how I came to obtain it. I still have my army pension after twenty-odd years.'

The tape kept on moaning away as I listened to him.

'Tin was discovered in that area in 1871. The mine opened in 1920. Water sluices were used to fix the ore on the open-cut mine. Surface mining continued for some time before the price of tin slumped in 1929. It reopened in 1942, funded by the government to assist the war effort, but closed again in 1949. The mine was connected to the Emu railway by the Waratah branch railway, which ran between 1900 and 1945.

'Dad, always the inventor, lived in a tent with all the amenities and made arrangements for his wages to be banked in Burnie. Mum could draw on it for her needs. Her dressmaking kept her busy. Dad rode home on his Lewis motorcycle each fortnight for a family get-together. The hundred-odd-mile stretch never worried him. In 1933, he joined up with a sawmill and in between used his skills as a carpenter building houses. My parents were always busy and so was I in study and sports. I had my eye on an eventual military career.

'Dad was always a giant figure in my life and I realise now that I was forever in his shadow. We're meant to take our own footsteps, because there are more sides of a mountain to climb. He had no right to die, but die he did, with the words of his beloved grandchild on his lips, "Paul", and he gave one last puff, and faded into that world of the undiscovered country. Mum had gone before Dad, slipping into dementia and becoming hard to get on with. Then in 1968 came the death of our son Paul as well.

'It didn't help Mary and me, as she retreated to a world of ranting and silence. Yet before some of those dramas she and I had some great moments. I inherited their house at Burnie, so I ended up with two houses and a shack and no loved ones left.'

Chocko filled me in with some of the history of the Jones folk.

'I'll attempt not to bore you, James, but just a few facts. Burnie's named after one of the lights of the settlement. It was surveyed by Henry Hellyer, who chose Emu Bay so as to give access to a port handy for further inland pastoral settlements. It was laid out in 1828. Timber was the main industry until tin was discovered. The convict (our relative) Richard Jones, who was transported a decade before, was later given a ticket of leave because of his mining expertise. Other Jones family members sailed out from Cardiff in 1857 and they all joined in building houses.

'Some of the forebears are traced back to the Isle of Anglesey, to the north-west of Wales. It was occupied by the Romans, who almost wiped out the population of Celts, priests and druids who were worshippers of the sun, the moon and nature and like choirboys compared to the slaughtering Roman army. Rumours still abound of magical powers of healing, not unlike the Buddhists and spiritualists of today.'

He told me that he visited an old relative, Auntie Mollie, who lived on the island and who read his cards: 'A marriage for you, my lad, and a return to your country.'

I intervened. 'Phew – that turned out right!'

He didn't respond with words but the black orbs did, with a withering stare. I felt like a person asleep during an opera who wakes up with a clap before the ending, with everyone shifting in their chairs wondering who the noisy fool was. I pulled out a cigarette and got it going with three flicks of the lighter and blew smoke through my nose.

Chocko was silent.

Still.

And then opened up. 'Give those devil things up. They'll kill you.' And after waiting for my reply, which never cam,e there was more. 'Remember *Hamlet*, son: "There are more things in heaven and earth than in your philosophy, Horatio."'

He went on with his history. 'Anyway, Dad limped back to Hastings with his gammy leg and a mind full of the charge at Beersheba on 31 October 1917 with the 4th Light Horse but with a regret haunting him about his beloved horse Traveller who would only let Dad ride him. In modern terms, he'd be called a horse whisperer.'

'Do you live between the two places now?'

'Yes, James. I'm not a hermit. I need to stay in the commercial world to sell my creations. So there's television, and a phone to stay in touch with the world. And of course I catch up with relatives, and go to the RSL Club.'

I turned the tape off and we went outside to breathe some fresh air.

4

MI5

'Okay, son, let's move on to Army Intelligence, of which there are two wings. Combat Int is where sources send in information which is turned into Intelligence and is collated, then disseminated to the operations room. Briefings occur usually on a daily basis. They're the map-makers. Then there's Counter Int, up to all sorts of tricks – agents, spies, assassins and just surveillance.

'I soon found out with a brief note containing an address with a day a date, a time and a place, that punctuality is the optimum for an aspiring agent. I was there on the button – not one minute early, not one minute late – and I knocked on the large old oak door which had survived the Battle of Britain. A panel of middle-aged men sat at a long table, some smoking cigars, some cigarettes. The man in the centre had a military moustache, a dazzling white shirt with an old-school tie – Eton – round a rugby-size neck. In my quick assessment I imagined that he might look like Walsingham, Elizabeth I's top spy.

'They were friendly enough, polite and yet precise with the preliminary chats, sussing me out to do a job of some importance, and I guessed it might have been in enemy territory, or close to the borders.

'"We read that your nickname is Chocko, and judging by the colour of your skin it seems to be appropriate, not that the colour of your skin is a problem to us and indeed it's the point of the mission, which we hope will be successful."

'I gave my widest smile and waited, hoping that the nerves came down a peg or two. The leader was frank and unblinking – I'm not bad at that either.

'His cultured Eton accent was to be expected. "Ever killed anyone?"

'There was a dilly-dally moment. "Not as yet, but I expect I will before the conflict ends."

'"I mean in cold blood, not in battle."

'I lowered my voice, yet still enunciating every word slowly, but containing my excitement and elongating certain words. I knew this was my leap into the big boys. I tried not to yell out, "Don't fuck this up, Chocko."

'"I know what you're saying, sir."

'"Hmm" was the short reply

'The group looked at one another with nods and hand waving and whispers in the room as if I was just an ashtray unmoving, something to be either lauded or squashed. They stopped the chatter as the leader passed a manila file marked SECRET towards me. There they were, waiting for a response, like a dog in water shucking off fleas. I opened it and read the text. A photo of a well dressed Arab man wearing the very best European clothes stood out. I had a darker complexion than the man in the file. I kept on reading without asking questions, because it was all there.

Ahman Casside, age 49 years, married with two grown-up children, originally from Jordan and a merchant worth millions.

'How did he get that much? was my thought. I looked up as the leader put his glass down on the desk with a bang, but I did not flinch and I reckon that was a little scenario to test my nerves. I wasn't going to fall for it.

'"Stage one: do you accept the mission? Stage two: to wear Arab clothing and change after into Western apparel. Stage three: a .25-calibre Beretta with silencer is to be supplied for the execution. Preferably a head shot if possible. Transport to be supplied, flexible for the conditions, back to homeland. Report at the conclusion to the number supplied."

'I had to struggle to take a deep breath and they knew it.

'"Up to it, Anthony?" said the leader, the first time he had used my Christian name.

'"Yes, sir."

'"Good. Here's the address of the pistol range. Attend there at 0800 sharp. Good luck. Remember we're at war and some of us have to do the dirty work."

'"Thank you, sir." I saluted and walked out.'

*

'I left on a plane bound for Casablanca with everything I needed to complete the mission.

'I pushed through the crowd of milling people in the markets dressed in the local attire and took a great gulp of air on the way and kept driving the oxygen deep into my lungs as was my practice every day. There was the address near the Casablanca shore. I rang the doorbell, which was answered by a pretty Arab woman in Western clothes.

'"Yes?" she said.

'"A parcel for Mr Cassside to be delivered personally." And for all to see, the sender's address was care of the German embassy.

'She waved me through and I thought, Yes, I know what side you're on, sister. Get in my way today and I'll plug you as well.

'She showed me the way up the stairs to the second floor. I never saw any security guards about. However, because Vichy France was vigilant, I opened the door after a knock. The man sat with his head down, writing, still speaking, not looking up, and held out his hand. This is a frequent event, I ruminated. I gave him the parcel. He was about three feet away and then I quickly drew my gun. He looked up the moment I fired straight into the centre of his forehead. He fell backwards on his chair and was no longer breathing.

'I walked around and opened his top drawer and saw a bulky brown parcel with the Nazi insignia and other letters. I opened the parcel, which had a large amount of Francs were in it. I didn't stop to count them. I went to the door, took off the robes and put them in my carry bag and walked down the stairs, into the sunlight.

'I was standing in a shelter when I heard a scream but I was soon on a PT boat, waiting nearby to ferry me to a submarine which would take me back to England. I had some dough which I would later use to open a bank account in the name of Mary Jones just in case I didn't make it home. The spoils of war were mine to keep, to build on back in Tassie if I made it through this bloody war.

'I dialled the number. '"It's done, sir."

'The educated voice was on the other end. "Good. Come to my office in two days. Did you see any Nazi papers about?"

'"Got a swag of incriminating stuff, sir."

'"You're in, Anthony. I knew you'd do it. Your name will simply be C."'

*

'And that's how I got the second part of my nickname Chocko From Morocco. How's that, James?'

I was flabbergasted, lost for words. This old man was an assassin. But it was war and a lot more atrocities were to be committed before the close of hostilities.

*

'The Battle for Britain had been won and the population gave out a selective sigh, though Dunkirk still lingered in the minds of the folk. I was in constant training in Scotland, enjoying better food than the masses. I was proficient in killing with a gun, a garrotte, a knife and my bare hands. I was yet to bump off someone with my hands, or a strangulation, and I found that the teams did not brag about the personal killings, but we all had bad dreams, as humans aren't wired nowadays to kill without conscience. At least that's what I thought.

'I've learnt to distance myself. I like walking in the silence of my solitude, seeing people as silhouettes against the sky. Conversations which sink into my inner being soon fade out without the fuel, leaving a faint click of sound at times. Is it solitude with an illusion or a delusion? I think at times that I'm quite mad. All I can do, if I get some spare time, is read a lot of books and prepare for another round of death, blood and bomb explosions.

'Like Dad, I'd had hands-on experience with setting dynamite, in the open-cut mine at Mount Bischoff. It could end up causing hearing loss, though no one in the team wanted to talk about it. The parachute dropped us in France on our mission of demolition. We carried out our tasks with great effects on the German railway system, taken over from the French. Somewhere along the line, either as a result torture or through payments, I bobbed up near the top of their hit list. Close calls were frequents but we were able to slip away.'

'After one explosion, an SS kid stepped out from behind a tree and started to fire as the team ran away. He didn't see me in the bushes with my radio. I made a wire loop and was on him in an instant. He kicked and tried to turn round but I had him. He gurgled, tried to call 'Mama' but to no avail and as his breath stopped I laid him in wet grass, grabbed his gun and ran off. We were short on ammunition, you see. I think that's the one incident that may worry me in my life. Still no rules in love and war, so they say.

'The third in command in the team kept butting in when we were briefed – just as goats do. He was told off by the team leader and told to shut up for a change. He reminded me of a hungry child with his nose pressed against the bakery shop window, wishing he could reach those sticky buns. I doubt if he was ever in uniform. Best suited to a storeman job where everything has to be perfect.

'In late December 1942, the leaders of the coalition of the brave slid towards me a file concerning a very serious mission in the port of Casablanca:

Port of Casablanca. ANFA Conference WWII. Prime Minister

Churchill and President Roosevelt arriving 14/1/43 for twenty days. Discussions on a US air base to be built near the bay to be a staging area for an eventual thrust into occupied territory.

'Phew, I whispered to myself, this is big.

'The same team leader, now without the butt-in goat man, told me, "Your mission, Chocko, is to mingle around wearing Arab clothing and get close as you can to the two dignitaries and watch for signs of terrorists. There may not be an insertion from the enemy but we have to be certain and take no chances. There will be visible guards about but sometimes they miss the target. We think you can add additional security with your speed and your training. OK for that?"

'"I'll do my best, sir.'

'I selected some other clothing before the trip to the bay. I travelled this time all the way by PT boat and the waters were calm. It tied up at the pier in the night for obvious reasons. The seaplanes bringing the leaders arrived as scheduled and cars carried the men to their meeting. The crowds were aware of this important moment for the city.

'I saw a man idling about looking very nervous and holding his belt. The cars moved off and the two leaders stood chatting and smoking, Winston with his usual cigar. And then I saw the man with the nervous look shuffle towards them slightly and so did I. He got close and then he pulled out a large knife and jumped in front of Winston. I disarmed him, the knife clattering to the ground. Military police rushed in and took him from my grasp. I showed them my ID and they moved away but security guards suddenly appeared and grabbed me. The bloody dopes had totally missed the action but they let me go when I showed them my ID card.

'Winston was sitting in the back of his car and seemed nonplussed. He winked at me and gave the V sign. He and Roosevelt were chatting as the car dove away.

'When I got home and stepped on the path outside the office, all those present clapped me as I went up the stairs.

'The leader was beside himself with joy. "Anthony, Churchill has recommended you for a DCM and the King will present it." He slapped my back and poured out a full glass of malt whisky, which I drank in one gulp. It had been a busy time.

'Months later, I bowed before the King, who also congratulated me as he pinned on my DCM.

'When 1945 came, I was still with MI5 in field operations. My team was unsure about our careers and it looked as though there might be some culling of staff. The IRA were up to their tricks and hated by the English. It was rumoured that German U-boats were able to sit in the harbours of Sothern Island. A fair amount of surveillance was conducted on known IRA members, particularly those who were bombers. They also had files on us, probably thanks to sympathisers within our ranks.

'A car was obliterated one night in a busy London street. The occupant was instantly killed. The bad news was all around the office the next day. It was Stephen Hayes, one of our own, who'd been raised in Belfast. He used to say that he was descended from one of the Welsh Warriors who Cromwell put on a seized property. It was owned by the Hayes for years. His killing was payback. He was a happily married man with children and we all felt the pangs of loss when he was buried with the Union Jack on the coffin. Some suspects' names bobbed up and we also found his notes from when he had shadowed one of the wanted men. I was chosen to target the bomber.

'He walked out of his business store one night and stopped to light a cigarette. The lighter was flicked a few times but didn't light. That was my chance.

'As I drew near, he asked, "Got a light?"

'I obliged him and then shot him in the head. He fell to the ground dead as a doornail, to use an old worn-out cliché. He bled in the gutter as I walked away. I hoped it was my last killing.

'The year ran away from us and I was putting in report after report requesting some home leave. Winston was thrashed in the election in the following year and Clement Attlee instituted his socialism, which worked for a while. I felt sorry for Winston but that's politics. The people wanted change and so did the unions.

'I was still at MI5 when I finally got a note saying leave had been granted. I flew home and met a kid who hardly knew me and some adjustments had to made. I was still in the army with the prospect of being hauled back to the group.'

'Family life went on and I was in Melbourne, mainly at a desk, and able to fly home a lot more, especially to watch Paul playing football and cricket. Mary and Paul were also able to travel to Melbourne and I set them up in my quarters. Paul was captivated with the pomp and ceremony of graduations and bands playing, and I also took him to our range, where he was able to shoot many weapons. That was the start of his eventual career – just like his father and my father.

'The Iron Curtain soon descended and we had a Cold War enemy on our doorsteps and the question of who could build the biggest bomb. Now a major, I kept my head down and expected that the younger men under my command might be promoted. Not so. 1950 came and so did Korea and guess what? I got another phone call from the old voice from the past.

'"Hi, Anthony. How are you? Your lad is growing."

'Jesus, they were still keeping tabs on me. Part of me wanted out but the past held me in the grip of forces beyond my control. I belonged to the world of power-brokering and the covert monitoring of citizens, though the buzz of it had left me. I knew I would soon have to return to a world from which I was powerless to escape.

'And that was a mistake, son, because I had handed over all control as a father and a husband, which in my opinion caused a permanent rift with Mary and Paul. I should have been there in that time to assist with all the little things which dads do, like my dad. Others were left to make critical decisions at those many critical times.

'The great love which Mary and I had just dissolved. Love is like water – it needs fresh material to sustain. So, James, don't let your career take over love. I should have just transferred to another corps, like medical, where I could undo all of my mistakes but still be with my family The two years sitting at the Korean desk buggered us up. Yet we stayed married.

'It was a mess, son. President Truman assumed that the first shot fired was by the Soviets. Wrong, and he didn't listen to the people on the ground. He directed a move by his troops, against his policy, into South Korea. He then knew that other nations should follow, so he called on the UN and other nations followed. During the war there were many charges that US Intelligence failed in the Korean War. Critics charged that US Intelligence didn't reveal the fact that the Chinese closed the border of North Korea.

'I was in Seoul at a desk and attending many useless briefings. I had enough. I requested a return to Australia and it was granted. I was soon back and trying hard to repair the damage to my marriage, which in my view was due to the long absence. This war wasn't like the last one. My time with MI5 was up, though I'm not sure it ever really is over.'

5

Family

'I can see by the way you're fumbling with the tape deck that we should give it a rest for while. I need my lemon and honey drink – Jane's home recipe – to clear my throat. Let's start again in a minute.'

*

'Right, let's talk about Mary, whose cool reception caused me to back off sometimes. Nothing seemed to work when I tried to be Mr Nice Guy. If she wanted another chair, I'd rush across the room and get it for her. A drink, I'd pour out a gin and lime – not good enough, too much lime. I'd iron my shirts, ask her if she wanted me to do some ironing for her – didn't like the creases. Feed the dog – he was too fat now thanks to me. I could go on endlessly. I spent more time fixing the garden as I had retired from the army and had to do something. Painted the fence – didn't like the colour. I read a lot outside.

'Like Mum, she was a great dancer but now it was a solo job in front of her fawning friends, who clapped after every jig. I made myself sit and applaud each move, which at last created a range of smiles. But a big competition was coming up and she confided in me that she was nervous. She was jittery and as pale as a person who has seen a ghost – and I've seen many in my life. I wondered if she was lingering too much on her old routine, which she had done a lot during the last few months, doing the right steps with turns and taps, kicks and leaps over and over in her mind, terrified that she'd forgot something, make a mistake, become lost and start to look like an idiot, like a woman who didn't know that she was dragging some toilet paper on her shoe and everybody laughed.

'It happened two years ago. Jane told me and said it was alcohol-fed. I knew that Mary was drinking heavily. I thought maybe she wasn't as good, yet she still had the moves – she still had the great body, which I loved, and when she was on a stage she was transformed. Some might say, "Who would notice the mistakes anyway?" but it was Mary on her stage, doing daring things so dangerous and so sweet that you couldn't breathe for watching her. Most of the audience were transfixed.

'After the final dance and the claps, she sat down beside me and, in a gesture which I hadn't seen for a long time, reached out and patted my hand. I laid my hand gently on hers and inwardly thanked God. I reached over and kissed her cheek and smelt the alcohol. She must have thought we were going too fast and jerked her hand away. And thoughts of some lovemaking faded away from the scene.

'She lost her balance on the way to the car and fell at the edge of the footpath. It was raining and the mascara ran into the heavy red lipstick. But I dared not say anything. However, Paul was sitting in the back and just shook his head. He knew a lot. I didn't think her habit was going away in a hurry and things did not get better.

'I'm told, son, that the definition of Insanity is doing the same thing over and over but expecting a different result. That applied to one of my attempts to heal the marriage. I took her out for a nice dinner in the town.

'While we waited to be served, her lips twisted into a leer. "Do you think I don't know what you're doing?" The words were delivered softly.

I thought about what she had said and it threw me, I had an inkling that a third person might have shared a life with her. I never broached the subject, preferring not to know .My parents never let on any gossip. Besides, who was I to judge? Jean the fighter in France and I had had some moments, until the Krauts arrested her and I never saw her again, which really put the icing on the cake for my hatred of those people. I sought revenge and got it in spades.

'"What do you mean, Mary?" I tried hard to be cool but my temper was getting close to an explosion and the place was full of people we all knew.

'"You just want to impress your friends. You want them to see us as the happy couple. But it won't work. That's why I'm wearing my red scarf – for danger. I took it from my mother's coffin years ago."

'With that show of paranoia, I knew we were on the verge of a separation. She needed help but there was no way anyone could ever attempt to encourage her to get medical help.

'We drifted away, with no hope of a reconciliation, son.'

I turned off the tape recorder and said, 'You're not on your own, Chocko. If we get a quiet moment, I'll tell you my story, if you'd like to hear it.'

'I would, son, I would. Tell me a bit of your story while the tape's off.'

'I think you said on the tape that you've seen ghosts. I saw one when I was fifteen. I was in my bed at Grandad Frank's house, where I lived. I was half asleep when I had a creepy feeling of being watched. I glanced up towards the window and watched the curtains gently swaying in and out even though there was no breeze. My caught breath would have woken the dead, as Frank was fond of saying, and there was a misty image of a slim man whose face was sort of familiar to me. He smiled at me and placed his hand on the windowpane, as though he wanted to come closer. I sat still, barely breathing. He was by then as visible as coal lying in snow. I threw off the blankets and ran fast down the stairs and woke Frank up and babbled on about a ghost whose face was familiar.

'Frank pulled out an old album and flicked pages. He gave it to me and said, "Turn the pages, James. See if you find a lookalike of your ghost."

'I did and there he was in a police uniform.

'Frank nodded. "It's your dad, James. He was killed in a motorcycle accident when he was quite young. He was a speed cop."

'I told him, "Mum never spoke about a father. It's puzzled me for years."

'"She was going to tell you at the right time. They were divorced and your mum shut him out because of the affair with a woman police officer."

'I had a range of thoughts running in and out of my brain in those micro seconds. About Mum's overdose, about the sad funeral and the missing times I should have had with her.

'Frank must have sensed my inner pain because he relieved my distress with the next words. "Your grandma and I loved her dearly and also your dad. Eileen died two years ago, as you know, and the silent grief just grew."

'I had another pressing question for Frank. "Why has Dad's ghost returned?"

'He said, "My guess is that he doesn't want to be forgotten. You may find in your life over the years he and your mum will return to heal the pain. We all have paid, James."

'So what do you think about that, Chocko?'

'It's a familiar story to me, son. Most people see ghosts but won't acknowledge that there's another world. I'd like to hear more of your story, son. Maybe after this you can come back for a holiday. We could do some fishing and meet some of the nice people around here.'

'Sounds good, Chocko. Actually my PTSD claim is about to be accepted. I propose to give up the job and concentrate on helping veterans who've been badly wounded in spirit.'

'That's a good path. Very noble. Time to tell you about Paul.'

6

Paul

'I kept a weather eye on my son and, in spite of the distance between his mum and me, he just got on with his life with his army studies and sport. The time rushed away with his entry into the army and finally the Engineers, in the footsteps of his granddad. Another demolition soldier. We attended his graduation and looked forward to catching up when some leave came. 1967 loomed. He'd been in Vietnam for a year and his posting was for two years. It's a year I'd rather forget.'

I noticed Chocko's skin turning a paler colour and asked him if he wanted to continue talking about Paul.

'I opposed the war and its propaganda that showed red arrows supposedly invading Australia. It was insufficient grounds for the USA to make that giant leap into that country. I considered that if the Western leaders had listened to the experts who knew the history of China and Vietnam, they would have left conflict well alone after the French were pasted. But with my position and career I was loath to speak up. In those days, people were not supposed to be whistleblowers. So there was my son, our only child, in high danger in a country which was being torn apart.'

I watched Chocko while he paused.

'The telegram came, delivered by the local postman. People were hanging over the fences and looking through curtains. It simply said that Corporal Paul Jones was killed in a helicopter crash and we were to be advised when his remains were returned to Burnie. I slumped and Mary screamed and rushed to the grog cabinet. That was that. Another young life wasted. Not even married – no kids, a short life. I can't claim I was proud as some used to say. The funeral came and there was no point opening the coffin. The Last Post was played and a flag was presented to Mary. I just walked away. 'It was the end for my wife. No more dancing, no more going out with her widowed friends. Her skin went yellow.

'The doctor came and after prodding here and there he took of his stethoscope and announced, "Liver cancer."

'Within the space of six months, I buried my wife and my son. I tried to look after Mary but she brushed away all my attempts and would only talk to Jane. I sat by her side in the hospital most days, occasionally falling asleep. I woke up one day with a start.

'Mary was staring at me with a sad look. "I love you, Anthony. I gave you a very bad time. Forgive me, please. Just hold me."

'I obeyed her wish and was stroking her hair when a rattling sound came. I stared at her. She closed her eyes and took her final breath.'

'I had fearful dreams after I laid Mary to rest. All sorts of emotions entered my brain, My usual walk around the block didn't work. Is our life like a piece of wet clay given shape by our every thought? I was in a deep dark cave standing in the mud of my life. Mary's death stumped me. I had nowhere to go and slipped into decadence for a time, until Dad pulled me out.

'The problem about Mary was that she constantly sought acceptance and while I was in Australia I provided the cheer-up words for her. My absence was the key, as she had lost the moral compass which I pointed for her on most days. I think her wild thoughts overwhelmed her and created within her a focal point on which to blame, which was men. Her heart became calcified due to the disappointment of not having her Sir Galahad about. But most soldiers in the war were away for up to fours years without any leave and the thought in my brain most times when I was overseas was, Get over it, Mary, and get on with it. Not much empathy on my part, and I'll take that burden to my grave, James.'

I had no comforting words for the old man, who by now had tears in his eyes. I thought about him as soldier, spy, assassin. And I was soon to hear about his final adventure as an activist. What a life.

My mind was not clear of the strife I had in the war in my marriage, which I couldn't save, so the best I could do here was to listen, enjoy the peace of the place and start thinking of what I could say to him. If I was asked at his point how my life was going, I would have said, 'My mind is full of nips and tucks, just like a slow-moving fellow getting a hurry up from a blue heeler nipping at my ankles. The nips hurt outwardly, he tucks lay inside, trapped like a closed oyster.'

In the morning when I open my eyes, I feel all my lumps and talk to myself. My arthritis is not as bad as others I know, at least I think it isn't. Other people's bodies become the measure of my own vitality, of the vibrancy of the life force within me. Sometimes I'm good. I think, shall I get up and go to the toilet? Shall I cook eggs for breakfast? No, too many carbs. Then I have to look in my special book for the carb counts. Time to go into my shed and do some wood carving. It usually takes me to lunchtime, and then out comes my carb book. I think I'm turning into a hypochondriac. Too many cooking shows – yes, that's it. Get some books to read from the library. Same old day, same old shit.

But if he decided that he wanted to hear some of my anecdotes, I might have to be selective about what I said, because they might bring in a range of emotions which could raise his already over-the-top blood pressure. Over these few days he has become my substitute Granddad Frank. I had to be careful where I went with this. I didn't want to lose another friend. With what he had done in his life, it was incredible that he had lived to seventy. He must have been kept here for a reason. As is said, frequently, God works in mysterious ways. Hey, that's funny, mentioning God now. Never did that much, although in a hole in the war, I called out at times, when the shells went whistling too close to our heads. I might ask Chocko what he thought about religion.

So much in life is aimed at either youth or near middle age. Almost nothing points us to the days when time alone will be our guide, our companion, our goal, our optimum. We have few or no promises about the glory of being busy, less harried, less consumed by everything. The later years of our lives are given to us to bring in the harvest of all that effort. We have learned so well how to live with the rules of life, we're not sure how to live in its freedoms. Yet I know some who live the freedom, some who have found escape to joyfulness. I know a lady who at age eighty-eight mows her own lawns, rides a bike each day to swim in an ocean, and ignores the signs about sharks. I think in time she'll become a shark's lunch. She won't care after the first bite into her lungs. After all, she has endured the pain of five childbirths.

Chocko From Morocco had, in a sense, that same fashion of ploughing on, a sort of damn the odds, live or die, whatever. If he stuck around for a lot more years, I hoped to emulate him.'

7

Jane's Dementia

'How's the tape, son? I'm about to venture into my mother's health –
another blow.'

I checked the tape and it was fine. He started with a preliminary
with the tape switched off and also had a sip of his mum's home-made
throat soother.

It was time to ask, 'Did you ever meet the James Bond author?'

He smiled. 'Ian Fleming? Yes, a couple of times. He had one serious
mission but he survived and I guess that's what started his writing
off. But enough of him. Back to my mum. I grew up in comfortable
surrounds in comparison to many people who lost jobs during the
Great Depression. Many men walked everywhere banging on doors
and asking if they could fix anything, chop wood, dig a garden bed.
My dad always had some invention up his sleeve and my mum was the
best dressmaker in the town, doing much for free, so you can guess she
was a popular woman.

'At the risk of repeating myself, she was born in France, lived in
England and could speak French, Spanish and some Italian, and I
grew up with other languages always in my head. If ever there was an
attraction law, it applied to my parents. I was privileged to witness it in
operation. Many people believe that the mind is like a magnet, which
picks up all sorts of sounds, thoughts and ideas, and what we hold
uppermost in our attention we attract to ourselves. Musicians know
this – it's called the principle of sympathetic resonance. Say you have

two pianos in the same room and you hit a C on one of the pianos ,
you'll find that the C string on the other piano starts vibrating at the
same rate. So much for the sceptics.

'After Jane went on the slippery slide, I did some research into
dementia. It becomes unstoppable like a freight train without brakes
and with her grandson killed in Vietnam and Mary dying with liver
cancer, the rot set in, in my opinion. Alzheimer's is the most common
reason for a person showing symptoms of dementia. Dementia means
loss of memory, decreased intellectual function and deterioration
personally. There are up to seventy causes of the disease, and the big
A is the most common. It's an actual physical disease of the brain.
Put quite simply, the brain is wasting away and losing its function,
resulting in the person's behaviour changing as the disease progresses.

'What happens to the person afflicted as the brain damage gets
worse? These are some of the effects: at first the brain copes, finding
mew pathways between the nerve cells as old ones become irreparable
but then the reserve cells pack up like a line of falling cards in a house.
The beginning of mental impairment affects every aspect of the person's
intelligence – imagination, communication, emotions, judgement.
Strange behaviour and lack of self-control all add to the process. The
whole personality is stunted but the person will look physically in good
health and that aspect can continue on late into the illness.

'With Mum, that was all true. Daily doses of medication helped,
though there were frequent times when she just stared blankly fixed on
an object near her vision. After the blank stare, she might muddle her
words – instead of "stare blankly" it might be "blare stankly", which
caused some behind-the-hand giggles.

'She became apathetic, lost interest in her dressmaking shop.
Daily walks were out. Friends were accused of stealing precious
items. A person with odd features, such as the bank manager with
bolting eyes, was called Barney Doogle. His secretary was called Miss
Prissy She greeted people with German names with the Nazi salute.
An overweight woman was called Miss Piggy and told to eat less fish

and chips. A woman who stalled her car was asked, "Who gave you a driver's licence?" The local cop with big ears was called Dumbo. I found her slippers in the fridge. Finally her hygiene started to wane and she smelled of decline. Poor dad was at a loss what to do.

'The last straw was when she opened the front door to the postman and was only wearing slippers. She dragged him by his tie into the parlour but Dad caught her in the act. The hospice came for her the next day. The postman didn't know she was gone and on his next visit stood back at least three yards, obviously still in shock at being nearly raped by a mad woman.

'There were tears when Dad and I explained that she had to go into care but we feared for her safety. After about two weeks, she came out of her state for a small window of time and signed the consent form. It was a tough day for us three.

'We kept her big secret – not that reading many spiritual books is a crime. Neither was her belief in a guide who used to talk to her and do what's called automatic writing. Hers was a bit different in so far as she believed the spirit talked to her through her old teddy bear named Charlie. In those tough days after Paul's death, she filled her diary with Q and A with Charlie. I felt like a thief intruding on her sacred thoughts but Dad had to see it. I'll read you some of what she wrote.

'ME: Hi, Charlie. Long time no see. Sorry about that.

'CHARLIE: No worries. Time doesn't exist here. It's past, present and future all rolled in together

'ME: It dawned on me after praying for some relief from my busy muddled life that I had to dampen down my grief about Paul.

'CHARLIE: You had to find a way to cope and to be happy with your role as a mother and a grandmother.

'ME: It occurred to me that my next chapter is to explore my disease and if possible write a book about it. Whether I have much more time on the planet is the question.

'CHARLIE: I can't tell you how long you have.

'ME: I've read a lot about God over the years. He has a sense of humour. I mean, fancy creating a platypus or a giraffe for a start, not to mention other strange creatures.

'CHARLIE: Just evolution, Jane.

ME: What about my treasured intellect? I think it's slipping down the drain.

'CHARLIE: That's a question which has dogged mankind for aeons.

'ME: Am I close to the final encounter and will I be with you when I reach that world?

'CHARLIE: I'll be with you when it's close

'ME: Bless you, Charlie.

'CHARLIE: And you as well.

'ME: One last thing: you remember the film *Casablanca*? Is Rick's Restaurant there?

'CHARLIE: No, dear. It's fiction, but you can meet Humphrey and Ingrid when you come over. Just call to them.

'Dad was in tears when he read the chats. I said, "She believes it. It's a pity that the rest of the world are just agnostic and believe in nothing but making money and treading over other people just to get on.

'Dad had lost his great mate, my mum, and the town mourned her passing. People read books from the local library to find out about the symptoms and whether they or their loved ones were on the slippery slide. Needless to say, the church was packed to celebrate her life and listen to the sobs, which included Dad's and mine. The family was shrinking. I'll never forget her for the rest of my limited days on this great plot of earth. I couldn't have had a better mum, and a friend.'

I sat staring at him until I eventually broke the silence. 'OK, Chocko, what's your take on love?'

He cleared his throat after downing a glass of water and began. 'I suppose what you're asking about is romantic love, which I call lovesickness. People in love may be threatened or possessed by jealousy and they find themselves the victim of another's need to control. They get stuck in a cold, abusive relationship, or fall into an impasse in which their love goes nowhere. They may feel they're with the wrong person, at the wrong time, in the wrong place and for the wrong reasons. Frequently, love doesn't work out, or rather goes stale. Some dream of passionate love, thrilling, sexy, others of a tranquil love with a tranquil life. The result may be a sharp turn into a nightmare. Love is also a kind of madness and it seems that one's in a bubble of fantasy where emotions are intense. They feel unbalanced and do silly things and a sense of responsibility disappears. Reasonable advice from friends and family has no effect. They refuse the advice – at their peril.' Chocko looked straight into my eyes in that moment.

All I could say was 'Bloody hell.' All those insightful words that came from experience in life. But I was not prepared to let other points of view slip away. My job was to wring out what wisdoms lay within in his brain, so I proposed another subject: creativity.

He opened up. 'People ask about my hobby, my art, my sculpture, I reply that it's simple: just start and keep going to the finish. It's more important, though, to create than to be a creator, in an inflated sense of the word. Creativity means to create, to add something worthwhile to the world. If you approach your efforts insecurely and uncertainly, your ego may get in the way and instead your focus will fix on being the creator. That is a backward step. Just start with something ordinary and creation builds. The idea is not to make you a star but to give your work the shine and sparkle that are signs of divinity.

'Real creativity is to be found not exactly in the middle, but in a mix of the ordinary and the special. The amounts of gratitude may vary for each person, but extremes serve no one. By nature, artists are thrown into a world of silence and it's not easy to be a creative person in this world which loves conformity. You must make an effort to live an original life, to avoid being carried along on a wave of cultural unconscious. In our insecure world, everyone wants to tell you how to think and how to live. But the high imperative is to forget rejections – they're part of the trade. How's that for a start, son?'

I just nodded.

8

Aborigines In Tasmania

'You're about to ask me a question, son. We have yet to discuss my activist life regarding the Franklin Dam, so speak now before we move on to that.'

'I've heard a bit about the massacres of the indigenous folk. What do you know about them and the resettlement on Flinders Island, I think it was.'

'Yes, because they wanted their lands, the settlers just about wiped them out for reasons like stealing sheep. A lot was done by convicts under the guidance of settlers and the army. The government decided to appoint a Chief Protector of Aborigines. George Augustus Robinson was selected even though he didn't have a blue clue about the Aborigines. He was there from 1839 to 1949. He had set up as a builder in Hobart in 1824 and his wife and five children arrived four years later.

'The conflict with the two cultures had vastly increased during the 1830s and became known as the Black Wars. Robinson investigated the Cape Grim massacre in 1828 and reported that thirty of the tribespeople had been killed. He became a conciliator between the warring groups. His mission was to round up the Aborigines and resettle them on Flinders Island. No beg your pardons, no asking if they wanted to live there, even though they'd been here for thousands of years.

'Most people weren't aware of the of the ancient caves. The area had hand stencils as well remnants of stone tools that were between eight thousand and twenty-four thousand years old. History was about to be destroyed.

'Robinson befriended Truganini, to whom he promised food, housing and security on the island until the situation on the mainland calmed down. In company with his new friend, Robinson succeeded in forging an agreement with the Big River and Oyster Bay peoples, and by the end of 1835, nearly all the Aboriginals had been relocated to the new settlement.

'His involvement with those people ended soon after that, though, and the settlement became more akin to a prison as conditions deteriorated, and many died from lack of proper food and from heartbreak. Robinson's name is mud on the pages of history. Of course the main mission of the settlement was a form of displacement and they either liked it or lumped it.'

'I guessed that, Chocko. Anglo Saxons have a penchant for colonising and wiping out indigenous folk. It has all the hallmarks of what the USA did to its Indians. I was always on the side of the Indians at the movies, as my parents were.'

'Time for some grub, son, and a bit of port.'

'Roger to that.'

9

Chocko the Activist

'There's a fair bit to say about the Franklin Dam controversy before I move on to the blockade, so stay with me, son. Okay, get yourself a port and relax.'

'Go for it, Chocko.'

'The Franklin Dam or Gordon-below-Franklin Dam was a proposed project on the Gordon River that was never constructed, The movement that eventually led to the project's cancellation became one of the most significant environmental campaigns in Australian history.

'The dam was proposed for the purpose of generating hydroelectricity. Construction would have had an impact on the environmentally sensitive Franklin River, which joins the Gordon nearby. During the campaign against the dam, both areas were listed on the UNESCO World Heritage Area Register.

'The campaign led to the consolidation of a small green movement that had been born out of the non-violent campaign against the building of three dams on Lake Pedder in the late 1960s and early 1970s. Between the announcement of the dam proposal in 1978 and the axing of plans in 1983, there was a vigorous debate between pro- and anti-dam lobbies. There were large protests on both sides.

'In December 1982, the dam site was occupied by protesters, and there were widespread arrests and greater publicity. The dispute became a federal issue in the following March, when a press campaign, supported by photos taken by Peter Dombrovskis, helped bring down the Fraser government. The new boys in Canberra under Bob Hawke promised to stop the dam being built. A legal battle between state and federal governments followed. The High Court ruled in favour of the Hawke government. So that's the background, son. Let's move onto the blockade.

'The conflict grew in 1982, when Bob Brown announced that the blockade was to commence on 14 December. Bob got to be the ringmaster. He had only been released from jail the previous day after spending nineteen days behind bars for his role in the blockade. My turn in the clink followed soon after.

'Throughout January 1983, around fifty people arrived at the blockade each day. I was one of that august body. The state government went out of its way to be nasty. They came up with new laws and enforced bail conditions. Over twelve hundred arrests were made, many for simply being present and watching. Five hundred people were jailed for breaking bail conditions. The jails were full to overflowing. British botanist David Bellamy was also jailed, as was John Marsden the author, and put in a high-security prison at Risdon for a night as there was nowhere else to keep him. A bloody great farce.'

I'd listened to all this words and had some questions. 'So, Chocko, how was prison?'

'Hey, son, I survived the tough course on being captured, mate. A lot better in the Tassie jail.'

'Cops treat you OK?'

'Hey, I was the oldest protester. I didn't reveal my MI5 years but someone found out about my medals and made up an album of photos that included the two French ones as well as my DCM, and all of a sudden I was a legend. But I ducked away after all the hoo-ha died down. You're the first one who's interviewed me.'

'I hope I've done you proud, Anthony.'

'Now listen. I want to hear about your life. You're a Vet, divorced. What do you say?'

'Okay then. What if I let you ask some questions and I'll put in a new tape which you can use.'

'That's good. I really would like you to come back soon so I can show you all of the distinct and we can take a cruise on my boat. How does that sound?'

'I can't wait.'

We had a great dinner of fish and I'd brought some white wine, which we knocked off.

10

James's Story

'Hi, Chocko. I feel that the whole of my life is a bit mundane. A lot of it is just anecdotes and not necessarily linear. You remember the ghost story I told you that Frank sorted out? Well, I thought I ought to start with his funeral, which I attended. Some surprising stuff came up afterwards about his war from one of his mates who came from Western Australia just to honour him. As a former soldier you might like it, I'm sure, and there are some stories about some of my war buddies which you'd appreciate as well. I'll fill in other bits as I blunder along. Stay with me on this journey, Chocko.

'I think there's a mutual fondness between us. You're like Frank, who became my father. That's why I feel the need to blow away the cobwebs of the past. Each hour that we communicate is a another milestone in my life.'

'Frank had his final heart attack and before I could summon up the faithful who knew and loved him, he was whisked away by men in grey, as quick as a north wind blowing in and taking the street debris to a marshalling point, where debris is sorted by the quick stubby fingers of men who have bags marked "rubbish", "good stuff", sort for recycling.

'Frank was soon polished up in the parlour, which was full of light and images of Jesus wherever I turned, soon to be sparkled, shaved with powder and paint which completed the process. The mourners touched the cask and whispered personal secrets while holding in their hands a sprig of rosemary for remembrance, though I believe that he would have preferred golden wattle sprigs, as he was a quintessential Australian.

'The pastor started out with the Lord's prayer – Granddad always made a joke of it by saying "Harold be his name" and I had to control a giggle. But it's not the time for humour just yet. We were seated and the chatter slowed down after the formal stuff from the pastor. A Cole Porter tune struck up just as the army chaplain walked in to do the rest of the spruik. He was Frank's battalion God man and he had a chest full of shining medals which clanked each time he waved his arms about to make a point. We stared at the screen and waited for the dot presentation to commence. Stills from the life of Frank followed in quick time but right in the middle, the overhead lights went out with a bang. We were in total blackness, except for green glowing dots on my army wristwatch.

'The silence was deafening and it reminded me of the quiet when in the jungle the birds stopped their chatter, the wind abated and the fear of the next charge had my heart thumping. I started to breathe deeply, sending the good air deep into the bottom of my lungs. My heart slowed to an easy pace, like the gentle rowing of a boat, with only the swishing of the oars to be heard. Sparks touched the top of my head, which caused dizziness. I felt faint and I reckon I was out for some seconds, unnoticed by my soon-to-be-separated wife Julie and our two kids.

'All the nightmares from my childhood danced before my eyes, all of the ghost stories I had read or watched at the movies. The stories told in the Boy Scouts while sitting around the campfire became giant shapes that darted to and fro like they were caught in a whirlwind. Those tales told of live people buried in a coffin with their nails shortened by scratching at the sides and unheard screams. That was the Sunday horror films – people rising from the earth, the sound of rubble thrown on the lids, skin peeling off their faces and ivory skulls with bolting eyes, like a surprised meerkat.

'Then bang again, the lights came on and we all blinked, but the dreadful images I had lived with continued when the coffin slid down, soon to enter a hungry fire which obliterated the man who had lived a full life.

'I was back again still upright on the cushioned seats and listening again to the speaker, watching the slides and hearing my two kids chatter. There were the comrades from Frank's war and, in front of me, was the Western Australian friend with rows of medals given to him by a grateful government.

'I followed John out and sat in the peaceful garden. I was bursting for any tales John could tell about Frank in the war and they came out one after another.

'"We were in Borneo and about to be charged by two platoons of Japanese marines, the shock troops of the army. Their shouts of 'Banzai' were so loud that they scared the birds out of the trees. But then it was still – eerie really – until their .25-calibre Woodpeckers rang out pop-pop. I can hear it in my nightly dreams and it won't go away. They ran towards us across a clearing and split into two groups. Five of them charged into our small foxhole. Frank jumped up and I saw a look of pure hatred on his twisted smile. He stuck his bayonet right through the guts of the lead soldier and threw him up in the air. The Jap screamed and wiggled like a fish caught, trying to break free of the long bayonet. Another one rushed at Frank, who grabbed him by the throat and strangled him with those large farmer's hands. He turned to the left and kicked an officer with a sword in the knackers. The fellow tried to get up on his knees but Frank grabbed his sword and swiped the fellow on the head, splitting the skull and dislodging brains and gore all over our great Sergeant Frank. There were the three dead Japs on the ground. Then he charges into the machine gun nest and ducks bullets and throws a grenade which kills them all."

'John stopped for a second and swallowed a butter menthol, licked his lips and went on with the story. "That's why he won the Military Medal. Most of us thought he should have got a VC but someone had already got one and that was the allocation. The bean counters, back-room boys, at it again."

'John licked his lips again. By this time a tear was running down his red skin, where patches of skin cancer showed through. "I still see it in my dreams as alive as us sitting here."

'John lit another cigarette and stood up but I was unable to rise because of my shaky legs and sat still giving a handshake and a wave to John as he lumbered away with his walking frame and disappeared around the corner to the waiting RSL bus now full of his comrades.

'I was transfixed, thinking about my tram driver carer named Frank Newton who always helped his neighbours, who loved his wife and me, who threatened a man who hurt his daughter, yet thought that God should have intervened to stop the carnage. I wondered then what he was thinking when he entered that distant other world. I thought about raw courage which must flow in when we're at full gallop, with not a moment to lose. It may come like an alarm clock at that exact time – not before, not after and only in tough times. But I knew that I would not have had the same courage and never showed it in my war. '

*

'I usually fall into a drug-induced sleep in the night and wake up feeling worse. Julie shifted into the spare room some time back, presumably because she had a fair bit of study in her social work job with the government, but she left her computer on by accident when she left early for work and I read on the screen a list of holiday resorts and a sea cruise to the Pacific islands, and a women's group which sprang out at me from another page by surprise.

'It led me into feeling that she was looking at making a new life for herself but I wasn't going to shirt-front her at that point, because it was up to her to come clean with me and then we could work it out. I hold loyalty to be paramount, and disloyalty is, in my opinion, unforgiveable.

'I entered the café on the way out of the bank where I used to work as a teller and there was a familiar face sitting at a table sipping his drink. He looked downcast. When I went to the toilet, it came to me in a moment: Clarrie Giles, from Vietnam.

'Clarrie was a signaller in our platoon and I got to know him very well before I was wounded. I heard after his Nasho was up that he returned to Telecom as a technician.

'"How are you doing, Clarrie?" I stuck my hand out.

'He stood up, pain wracking his face, and quickly sat down again. "Bloody James Newton, as I live and breathe. Heard you were wounded in '67. How are you?" he added.

'It was in my mind to just lie and say the traditional "Just fine" but I changed my mind for some unfathomable reason. "Lots of aches and pains but the old Panadol works a bit. Had problems with the work at my father-in-law's business but that looks like folding as he and his wife aren't getting on, but got a problem with the missus, mate – not sure where it's going."

'"It's a big club. I joined up sometime back. Two divorces since we met and can't get it right with the other sex. Bloody Vietnam – got to blame something."

'"No more marriages for me. Julie's the love of my life, but I don't think that applies with her."

'Clarrie passed over some coin and said, "Get two coffees and sit down after. I'm all ears."

'I spoke about what I'd read on her computer and he listened intently. "So tell me, Clarrie, what's your life like? Not happy, I guess, if I'm any judge of facial expressions."

'He swallowed his drink in one gurgling minute while I watch his Adam's apple jumping up and down. He asked for another drink, which came to our table within seconds.

'"My situation has gone beyond repair. My job went west after Jenny decided she wanted to be a lesbian."

'I sat back as a result of his revelation, my eyes as wide as the bottom of a whisky glass. I got control of my thoughts. A tear drifted down his face and stopped at the skin graft on his jaw line.

'It didn't stop him telling me all of his problems. "I'm a basket case now. First the job, then the wife packs her bongos. We didn't have kids, thank God. The house went. because she borrowed money for the bloody pokies and in my name for Christ's sake. I didn't have a wage coming in and the bank foreclosed on the house. Precious things started to go. All in an old box to a thrift shop. Our dog and cat went to the stray animals place to be put down the next day, which really broke my heart. I felt like drowning her but she's a big as a country shit house and it wasn't feasible. Eventually the car went and so did she – bitch." He stopped and wiped the dribble off his lips.

'"Surely there's not more, Clarrie?" I thought, what else could there be, except death?

'"Try motor neurone disease, mate.'

'I was flabbergasted. And he stopped staring in my face. It was akin to a comedy. So sad, like the biblical Job and his trouble with God.

'"So what have you got to worry about, James?"

'I couldn't come up with any comforting remarks so I reverted to what I could do for him at that moment. "Can I give you a lift anywhere?"

'He shook his head and replied, "The van's picking me up but thanks for listening to my story of woe." He thrust out a card saying where he would be.

'I was damn sure I would stay in touch, not like I was with Frank, when I got too busy to keep up the visits. Of that I was well and truly ashamed.

'The hurdle with Julie had to be faced and soon. I steeled myself for it, determined not to crack. I took my meagre breakfast out onto the patio just before I went to work in those closing days and I watched the birds picking up the crumbs, which is a pleasant thing to do. I thought there was a lot more of nature that I would embrace one day but right then I was going to embrace sadness, spliced with Tom's plight, told to me with that Australian humour sense misting in the air.

'The leaves were falling off the maple tree, some of the leaves clinging onto life and not dropping, just changing colour. The wind blew some away that landed at my feet. Others were scooped up down the street to neighbours who used them for mulch. I imagined the leaves if they could speak saying, "Well, we've had a good life and now it's time to go. Evergreen next time, eh?"

'I heard Julie smashing around in the kitchen, which she always did when she was in a shitty mood, which was a daily happening of late.

'I called out to her, "It's marvellous. Come and look outside. The leaves are changing colour right before my eyes and landing at my feet."

'"I'm busy reading."

'"Leave the paper for later. The leaves won't wait for tomorrow." I sat waiting for another arrogant answer but the wait was in vain.

'"I have reservations."

'I'd read her reservations but could not remember which crowd she'd be travelling with. I played dumb in those seconds. "Going out?" Gee, I'm getting smart. I was starting to enjoy this little bit of tit for tat. "Stop, James. This is serious," I murmured.

'"A plane actually., You know, one of those big things with wings and painted with silver, makes a lot of noise."

'Sarcasm. Okay, two can play that game. "Where to on this big thing which is silver which makes a lot of noise and has big wings and smells of petrol?" Take that, bitch.

'"Anywhere out of here."

'I was now the trout fisherman and I was going to get my best fuck-you chess piece in on this little bit of who won.

'"I thought you liked it here?" I shoved that one in because I was not only fishing but I wanted to let her know that she was not the only one in charge. My spirit surged while I waited for her response. I knew the outcome.

'"It's not the house. It's you."

'I looked at her with my best dazzling smile and said, "You're off on a cruise with your female group."

'A shocked look spread across her face and I enjoyed another bit of closure. "Feel free to go. As I will be to live my life."

'She had no answer, and just stood there with her face drained of colour. I stood up and walked out the door to go to work and called back, after looking at a her car, "Your front tyre's flat."

'I walked out and backed out of the garage. I – the man who normally did everything around the place – was leaving her to her own devices, she who had never known who to call to fix the many things which could go wrong in a house. I resigned from her dad's business and did a journalism course, as you know, Chocko. And there's a few more anecdotes for you.

'Ralphy became my friend and saviour during our national service in Vietnam in 1966. I met him in the army medical rooms when we went through our tests. We passed with flying colours and it was soon off to the initial training camp in Victoria. The trip with the army to bolster the ranks was set for two years. Some made it without injury, some were discharged with mental problems and some never returned. I reckon five hundred were killed, some by friendly fire and some by the local jungle diseases. Ralphy and I were assigned to the same platoon and within the rules of the army we were to buddy up with others. Ralphy was considered to be officer material but it didn't happen in those two years.

'He was what was called a God-botherer but I never saw any sign of his toting around a Bible. It was just when we were in a tight spot that people who were agnostic asked him for help and he freely gave it. In our jungle training in north Queensland, he shone and was always there to help the guys who struggled on the climbs and the jump from high into a great lake brimming with the local fishes and of course the dreadful ticks, which Ralphy skilfully removed from toes and legs. We wondered where his skills came from and guessed it must have been from a tough life in the bush. He was fostered and never knew his parents, which could make or break a child. In his case, he survived and applied himself during all those school years. He topped the platoon at the warfare centre in Canungra The instructors couldn't speak highly enough of his mental and physical skill. He was to be the ultimate soldier.

'Yet with all that ability, he remained a private right through our tour. We watched other guys who weren't bursting with ability make it to corporal within a short space of time. However the war areas were not a place for promotion by just mere paperwork achievement.

'Our war was a mix of hard work, boredom and letters from home, some leave, some action with an enemy who always came on with a rush when we were least able to cope. And how quickly we thought, the VC could disappear back to their tunnels. But cope we did and learn we did. However some mates were killed when, outside the safe area, they forgot the passwords. And also some were wanking out in the bush. After all, they were young men at the height of their sexual prowess and many had willing girlfriends in Australia. I don't forget the US artillery, which dropped shells about a bit too close to our lines, which would have caused some amusement among the VC. Some guys got the clap from bar girls in Saigon and were sent home to try to explain to their girlfriends.

'In quiet times back at the base, the guys opened up to Ralphy and let him speak about his beliefs and most of them agreed that he was smarter in many areas than the rest of us. He used to say, "I don't harass people. I'm not an evangelist. If people want to know what I think, they can either accept or not."

'Jack, the usual quiet one who just listened rather than making comments asked, "Do you worry about criticism? I mean, this is a cynical war?" And he added, "The warrant officer reckons he's a sceptic."

"I just avoid discussions with sceptics. Not worth the trouble, Jim."

'Richard hit the nail on the head. "What about the killing we do?" Richard looked pensive as he waited for a reply and scraped his foot in the sand at the same time.

"History is loaded with everyone praying to God for a win. Hard to answer." Ralphy went into his take on wanting to be popular and it sounded like something the Buddhists would say. "The need to be popular can in time make you neurotic and steal your destiny on this earth. You become a puppet hanging onto everyone's words and bound to fall down the track."

'My mind was racing to catch up. I added my own takes. "Like a mountain climber whose last spike slips."

'The guys were quiet, looking at one another about my sudden metaphor.

'Ralphy reacted to my words. "I suppose so, James, but like the climber he has faith or maybe just simple trust, not certainty." He paused again. "It's just really trust for all of us here in this moment."

'Two weeks later, I was in dire need of just trust when we were ambushed in the night and felt a searing pain in my leg and shoulder. Screams came from somewhere and then I knew it was me. The chopper picked me up with other soldiers who were dead and I was soon in the base hospital with visitors eating all of my goodies and bananas. But not Ralphy. He brought a lot of stuff in, and a Bible, signed by him. I must read it one day.

'I was recovering and walking a bit with a frame when Ralphy walked in one day.

'He had something to tell me and showed me his old birth certificate. "Have look at his line. What do you read as mother?"

'I looked and there it was: "Part Aborigine."

'The next thing he said was "Does that worry you, James?"

'I got a bit bothered that he should think it would change me and told him so and he just nodded. There was stillness, with his thoughts all over the place.

'I broke that stillness. "Hey, Ralphy, this explains a lot: your great running ability and your amazing long sight, and you can kick a footy seventy yards. Lead me to it. If I could do what you do, without hesitation I want to be an Aborigine.'

'He laughed out loud and so did I.

'I was repatriated to the base and then to Melbourne, where my time was occupied with checking stores. My tour was over and I was okay. Ralphy stayed in the army, found his birth secrets and married He became a warrant officer. Sadly, he died a short time ago. I missed his funeral.'

*

'I met Julie at a dance and we fell in love. Her father offered me a job in his big accountant outfit. We were married in a sumptuous celebration and two kids came along. But I always thought I didn't fit in, which was proved right, as I've already told you.

'A few years before we hit that hurdle, I was shopping in accordance with a message from Julie. We'd chucked out all the dried-up packaged food which was blocking the freezer. In the process of surfing different items on display, I smelt a pungent odour behind me. I turned and saw a dishevelled man with lanky greasy hair and an uncut beard. He shuffled as though his feet were sore and carried stained sheets under his left arm.

'I studied his blinking eyes as he moved towards the checkout, walking by the tinned food. He grabbed tins of sardines and put them in the deep pockets of his old ragged trousers. Passing patrons were ducking from him as he moved around the store. The air conditioning came on throughout the store, which made the atmosphere so unbearable that some customers had to go outside.

'He reached the checkout counter and pulled out a crumpled five-dollar note. It wasn't enough.

'The rather rude assistant held her nose and said, "You need more."

'I pulled out a five-dollar note and put it on the counter. I reacted to her curt words which were not necessary. "Nobody knows why he got into this state. You ought to improve your manners,' I growled and followed the man out of the store into the fresh.

'All the waiting patrons rushed back to their unfinished shopping.

'There was something about the man that made me increase my pace so that I could catch up with him. He stumbled across the park and it was getting dark. I was still on his heels and determined to find out if I knew him.

'A woman with two kids in a pram hissed at him when he brushed past, "Watch it, slob," she yelled.

'He vanished into the thick bush.

'Two young cops were searching the bush and a police dog was sniffing around excitedly, hardly able to contain his excitement about a parry nearby. They found him under a crumpled plastic cover. He stood and turned round. I recognised him as he was well known for his death stare.

'It was a moment I would never forget when I said to the cops, "It's Tony Wright. We were in Vietnam together."

'The two young cops whispered and then looked at each other when his undercoat revealed two stripes and military ribbons.

'"Look, we'll have to take him in and get him cleaned up. Can you come back in two hours?"

'I confirmed that and told them I'd pay for any stolen goods. He was whisked away.

'I went back on time and hardly knew the cleaned-up man. "Remember me, Tony – James Newton?"

'His face was blank for a second and then he whispered, "James."

'Conversation was limited. The sergeant rang the store and explained it all, and that the goods would be paid for. The store did not press charges.

'"Come with me, mate. You can stay at my house."

'He walked with me to the car and when we were near he darted off into the night. I searched for him but it was too dark. I didn't heard any more about his whereabouts until the sergeant spoke to me on the phone.

'"Sorry to tell you, James, Tony hanged himself last night."

'I was sad but knew there were unresolved mental problems. His wife had left him. He'd lost his job – not through any misdemeanour just a close-down. I went to his funeral and wondered if he had moved into the ether of that undiscovered country. He was a Catholic and suicide is not on their books. A Salvation Army chaplain took over. He had been a good soldier and I found myself thinking about his end. And his wife who decided to pack up and go. I was not in the mood for judgement as I didn't know the circumstances. Poor Tony still bobs into my dreams on occasions.

'I've read a lot of spiritual books since Julie went. I felt a need to be with like-minded folks and soh I joined some spirit groups who included yoga as an aid. However, the arthritis makes it difficult to get my body into those awkward positions, so I really stay as much as I can in the writing.'

'You've done a lot for people, James.'

I nodded and took a swig of his grog.

'"We remember our mates. Most of mine are long gone, son. What is the meaning of life? Just observing every second, I think. Don't search for the meaning. It's not under a rock or in a cave. Just move on, always noticing, and if you die in the process, well, that's cool. At least you didn't die in a state of boredom." That was Chocko's homespun take on life.

'So Chocko, I hope you'll read my article. I hope we can spend the rest of my time here, as you promised, with a trip up the Arthur River, finding Tasmanian devils, catching fish and collecting driftwood. And finding the great trees, in the environment you were arrested for trying to save. I'll drive into Burnie and post your story, as Bill's breathing down my neck. I'll have some news for him about me quitting soon.'

11

Chocko's Last Act

True to his word, three weeks after I returned to Melbourne, Bill published the Chocko's story of in the weekend magazine and it received rave reviews. I sent a copy of the magazine to him and received the news that he was in a hospice.

When I called him, his voice was faint. A tear came into my eyes when he said, 'Bless you my, son.'

The nurse took over and said, 'Chocko is sending you a big envelope with some good news for you. He says you deserve it.'

I flew over to his funeral and sat stunned at how the church was totally filled. Engrossed in my thoughts of those conversations we had which stretched into dawn, I sat there hardly hearing the words of the padre. One conversation had stuck with me.

'Do humans ever understand life while they live it?' I asked him.

'No,' he said. 'The saints and the poets, maybe – they do sometimes.'

I looked back on my life and recognised the tragedies of small splendours lost each day. I had been too anxious, scurrying to and fro so fast with no time to look and smell the roses.

I pondered about the time we shared. Short as it was, I learnt a lot from the man. I'm weaning myself off the accomplishment saga which is another rung on the ladder that I can't reach. I'm done trying to get my worth and value out of being perfect so people will admire me, or even that I'll admire myself. That was why the missus and I headed in different paths

Worrying about a halt to aspirations is like rocking back and forth in a rocking chair all day long: it keeps us busy, but it gets nowhere. I've lived my life forward; sadly, I can't understand it backwards. So what do I do from now on? Just get a block of wood and shape something. Yes, I say to myself, there is a key there for the rest of my life. My old mate did the same. I'll follow his lead.

I shake myself back into conscious as I whisper to Chocko, 'I'm here, old mate.'

*

The pastor said after the funeral, 'He's our own legend.'

I agreed with him. But all the way through the flight back, I reread the news in the envelope.

Simply put, he left me in his will the shack and contents. And the ute and the boat. He hoped that I'd stay and live in the shack. His generosity extended to his house in Burnie, which was left to become a safe house for women and children subjected to family violence.'

'Good for you, Chocko. I'll soon be obeying your wishes.'

I remember just before I left him he held my shoulders tight and whispered in my ear his mother's favourite words from *Casablanca*, 'Here's looking at you, kid.'

As I walked away with his last words ringing in my ears, I thought about the last scene in *Casablanca*, when the plane warming up. I remembered the last parting words from the once lovers

Ingrid Bergman as Isla says, 'Well, Rick, we always have Paris: Do you remember Paris?'

Humphrey Bogart as Rick replies, 'I remember every detail. You wore blue: the Germans wore grey.'

Epilogue

True to his word, James moved to Tasmania and now lives in the shack which Chocko bequeathed to him. He intends (with council approval) to add two more bedrooms at the rear of the workshop. The Driftwood Society attends on a monthly basis. He has many friends in the area and subsequently his social life has become a turn-up for the books. There are a few Vietnam veterans living the area: he meets with them at the Burnie RSL.

He also has a friend whose husband died after wandering off with PTSD into the bush. He supports cancer for children foundations and has also acquired a blue heeler dog, who loves to ride in the boat each Friday. He has named the dog Astro.

A DVD sits alongside the gramophone. He has a copy of *Casablanca*, which is loved by the older folk, who can't get enough of Rick. And he plays the soundtrack LP for visitors.

He believes that Chocko keeps a weather eye on him at all times.

About the Author

Ray Clift lives in Adelaide, South Australia, with his wife Ann, who is an avid reader and an excellent cook. Between them they have several grandchildren. Ray writes, walks and plants native trees. His forty-seven years in law enforcement with the South Australian Police and the Courts Administration Authority, plus fifteen years in the Australian Reserve Forces, Army Intelligence, and a few years with the Military Police, provided a bucketload of experiences, which have enabled him to write sixteen books published by Ginninderra Press, who can be contacted at www.ginninderrapress.com.au. Ray's books are available in print and ebook editions from Amazon and other online sellers. He he loves *Casablanca*.

www.ingramcontent.com/pod-product-compliance
Lightning Source LLC
Chambersburg PA
CBHW020347110726
47898CB00003B/1073